PAEONY LEWIS

Cinderella's Wedding

Illustrated by Ross Collins

MACDONALD YOUNG BOOKS

Chapter One

"Only two weeks to go before we're married," said the Prince to Cinderella, as they strolled in the palace gardens.

"I wish it were today," said
Cinderella. "What would we do if
something terrible stopped our
wedding?"

The Prince kissed the dainty tip
of Cinderella's nose.

"Nothing will stop our wedding,"
he said. "Not even your horrid sisters."

"My sisters have stopped being
horrid. Ever since the glass slipper
fitted my little foot, they have been
so kind," said Cinderella.

The Prince raised an eyebrow. "At the dress shop, was it kind of them to lock you in the toilet all day? And another thing, when I offered to pay for your sisters' dresses, I didn't think they would choose twenty each."

"I'm sure the toilet door was an accident. Oh dear. Are you cross about the dresses?" Cinderella's big blue eyes started to water.

"Of course not." The Prince plucked a red rose for his dear Cinderella.

Cinderella smiled. She loved the Prince, and the Prince loved her. What could possibly go wrong?

Everyone called Cinderella's horrid sisters Hiccup and Nosy. They never listened to anyone, so they never knew.

"I can see that silly Cinderella," said Nosy. She was watching the royal palace through a hole in the fence.

"Let me see!" said Hiccup. She tried
to push Nosy out of the way.

"Ged off! This is my hole," said
Nosy. "Oh, yuk! The Prince has given
Cinderella a red rose."

"Hic!" Hiccup hiccuped. "When I marry the Prince, I shall insist on gigantic diamonds, not soppy roses," she said.

"What are you babbling about? *I'm* going to marry the Prince," said Nosy.

"No, me," said Hiccup. "Hic!"

"Me," said Nosy.

"No, me," said Hiccup.

"Me."

"No, me."

"Me."

"No, me. Hic!"

"Get out of here!" roared a royal guard who had come to investigate the noise. "And *Cinderella* is going to marry the Prince," he added.

"No, she's not," said the horrid
sisters, and they stomped off together.

Chapter Two

The horrid sisters started plotting. They were sure one of their sneaky plans would make the Prince fall in love with them. (They decided to argue later about which one of them would marry him.)

Plan Number One was Nosy's idea. They would send the Prince love poems.

"I'm a real poet," said Nosy. "Listen to this..."

Roses are red,
Daisies are not.
Our teeth may be black,
But Cinderella talks rot.

"That's nothing," said Hiccup. "The Prince will beg me to marry him when he reads *my* poem."

We love your castle,
We love your money.
We love your servants,
We love your jewels.
We love your horses,
We love your chickens.
What more could you want?
Please love us too
(and not that silly Cinderella).

The Prince showed Cinderella the love poems.

"Aren't my sisters funny?" said Cinderella, giggling. "And these poems must have taken them ages to write. How thoughtful."

The Prince smiled and sighed.

Hiccup came up with *Plan Number Two*. Both sisters baked biscuits for the Prince. He was sure to fall in love with their yummy cooking.

"Ouch! I've cracked a tooth," wailed the Prince.

He threw the tin of biscuits across the palace floor. They skidded to a stop by the royal dog.

Cinderella ran and gave the Prince a big hug.

"Your sisters' cooking is terrible," said the Prince.

"Yeowl!" said the royal dog. He, too, had cracked a tooth on a chocolate chip cookie.

CRACK!

Cinderella ran and gave the royal
dog a big hug, too.

"I'm sure they were only trying to
be kind," said Cinderella.

The Prince and the royal dog both
sighed.

Nosy was sure that *Plan Number Three* couldn't fail. The horrid sisters sent the Prince a pair of Cinderella's old socks. They were really smelly! That would put the Prince right off her.

Cinderella was walking the royal dog in the palace gardens, when the parcel arrived.

"I'll take the parcel to the Prince,"
said Cinderella.

The royal guard took the peg off his
nose. He was happy to get rid of the
smelly parcel.

"I'm sure I recognize that smell,"
said Cinderella.

She let the royal dog have a sniff.

"Woof, woof!" said the royal dog.

"Yes, it is a nice cheesy smell," said Cinderella.

The royal dog snatched the parcel and ran off. He ate the socks. They tasted much better than the chocolate chip cookies.

Plan Number Four was Hiccup's idea –
singing love songs to the Prince outside
the Palace windows.

"When I sing, everyone stops to
listen," said Hiccup.

"The Prince will fall in love with my
beautiful singing," said Nosy.

"Guards!" roared the Prince. "There
are wolves howling outside my
window. Get rid of them!"

Slosh! A bucket of cold water soaked the singing sisters.

Hiccup and Nosy went home.

"At least we won't need a bath this week," said Hiccup. "Hic!"

Chapter Three

"What's *Plan Number Five?*" asked Nosy, as they climbed into their beds that night. "Time's running out – it's the wedding tomorrow."

"It's your turn to think up a sneaky plan," said Hiccup. And after one last hiccup, she fell asleep.

In the middle of the night, Nosy
jumped out of her bed. "I've got it!"
she cried.

"Got what? A bed bug?" said
Hiccup.

"No, stupid. I squashed the bugs
before I got into bed," said Nosy. "I've
come up with a brilliant plan. It's
unstoppable." Nosy was so excited,
she couldn't stop scratching her nose.

Hiccup listened. Hiccup became so excited she couldn't stop hiccuping. It was a brilliant plan.

Plan Number Five was very sneaky indeed. Hiccup had the best handwriting, so she wrote the letter:

Dear Cinderella,

It's bad luck for us to see each other just before the wedding. I'd like you to get ready at your beautiful sisters' house, they'd love to see your dress. Love Prince X

"Put some more kisses at the bottom," said Nosy.

"Yuk!" said Hiccup and she quickly stuffed the letter in an envelope.

Hiccup leant out of the window to see if she could see the postman. There he was.

"Oi! Postman! Come here. Hic! Take this letter to Cinderella, and no dawdling."

She slammed the window shut.

"Now all we have to do is wait for that silly Cinderella," said Nosy. "Then we can lock her in the cellar, steal her wedding dress and veil, and I shall go to the wedding and marry the Prince in her place."

"No way!" shrieked Hiccup. "Hic! I'm going to marry the Prince."

"*Plan Number Five* was my brilliant plan," said Nosy.

"I wrote the letter," said Hiccup.

"I'm the most beautiful," said Nosy.

"A rotten cabbage is more beautiful than you," said Hiccup.

"You smell like a rotten cabbage," said Nosy.

"I've got an idea," said Hiccup. "What if I give you my entire collection of funny-shaped carrots? Will you let me marry the Prince?"

Nosy scratched her nose as she thought about this. Hiccup did have some wonderful carrots in her collection.

"I'd want your jam-jar collection too," said Nosy. "And all your party dresses."

"Hic!" Hiccup thought about this. "Agreed," she said.

Chapter Four

That afternoon there was a knock
at the door.

Hiccup and Nosy opened the door.

"Hello," said Cinderella. "I'm getting married today. Isn't it wonderful? I'm not supposed to see the Prince before the wedding, it's bad luck. But he did send me a lovely note." She smiled a dreamy smile.

"Where's your dress and veil?" demanded Nosy.

"Here they are," said Cinderella. "Aren't they beautiful?"

"Yeah, lovely. Let me help you with that heavy dress," said Hiccup, and she dragged it off Cinderella.

"You can get changed in the cellar," said Nosy, and she pointed down the steps.

"It's very dark down there," said
Cinderella.

"You'll look much better in the
dark," said Nosy. She pushed
Cinderella down the dirty cellar steps
and bolted the door shut.

Nosy helped Hiccup squeeze into
the dress.

"It looks a bit tight to me," said Nosy. "I think I'd better wear it."

"Ged off!" shouted Hiccup. "It's a perfect fit. Hic!"

Nosy threw the veil over Hiccup's head.

"That's better," she said.

"I'm off to get married!" said Hiccup. "Hic!"

She went outside to Cinderella's carriage and drove off to the wedding.

Chapter Five

At the church, the pews were packed with lords and ladies. The Prince stood there, waiting. Hiccup started to walk down the aisle. Soon she would be a princess.

"Hic!" Hiccup was so excited she started to hiccup. "Hic! Hic!" She couldn't stop hiccuping.

The royal dog growled as she
walked past.

"Hic! Hic! Hic!" The nearer she got
to the Prince, the louder the hiccups
became. "HIC! HIC! HIC!"

Hic!

"What's wrong, Cinderella?" asked the Prince.

"HIC!" Hiccup gave such an enormous hiccup her veil blew off.

"Arrrgh!" yelled the Prince, when he saw he had almost married Hiccup, and not Cinderella. His yell was so loud the shock stopped Hiccup hiccuping.

"Listen, my hiccups have stopped. Hurry up. Let's get married," said Hiccup.

"Arrrgh!" The Prince yelled again, even louder.

"I'm much nicer than silly Cinderella, and I'll look after all your money for you," said Hiccup.

"ARRRGH!" yelled the Prince, again and again and again.

"Well, if that is all you can say then I don't want to marry you either," said Hiccup. And she flounced out of the church.

Once the Prince had stopped yelling, he rode off and rescued Cinderella from the dirty cellar. She did feel silly for falling down the steps.

"How kind of my sister to rush to the church to find you," she said.

The Prince raised an eyebrow and sighed. He didn't tell Cinderella the truth – he didn't want to spoil the wedding.

So, did everyone live happily ever after? Well... sort of.

After a good wash, Cinderella and the Prince were married later that afternoon. So they were definitely happy.

Nosy had Hiccup's collection of funny-shaped carrots, jam jars and party dresses. So she was a bit happy.

And Hiccup? She never hiccuped again. So she was a tiny bit happy.

Oh yes, the royal dog was happy too – he ate all the wedding cake.

Look out for more exciting new titles in the Shooting Stars series:

My Dad Is... by Ali Ives

When Becky Harris has to write an essay about her dad, she has a huge problem. She doesn't have a dad! So she decides to make one up. First she pretends that he's a doctor, then a chef, then a photocopier salesman, then an actor, but none of her dads seem to be quite right. What is she going to do?

Never-ending Birthday by Mary Hooper

It's Jamie's favourite day of the year – his birthday! All day long, he's spoilt rotten. He wishes it could be his birthday every day. But when Jamie's wish comes true – again and again and again – it starts to drive everyone mad. It's up to Jamie's friend, Meera, to sort things out.

You can buy all these books from your local bookseller, or they can be ordered direct from the publisher. For more information about the Shooting Stars series, write to: *The Sales Department, Macdonald Young Books, 61 Western Road, Hove, East Sussex BN3 1JD*